SANTA POST

SANTA'S GROTTO

BY EMMA YARLETT

There were only five sleeps until CHRISTMAS when...

WHOOOSH!

Something fell down Santa's chimney.

It was some very late SANTA POST. Who could it be from? Santa pulled it out and opened it up.

* Santa Claus,
The grotto, *
☆ North Pole

the letter. It was a PROBLEM. A BIG PROBLEM.

Santa tried to work out what Amy wanted for christmas for hours...

and hours and HOURS! But he needed help.

Extra special North Pole help - and FAST! "I'll write to Head elf Elfalfa," he said. "She will know what present to give Amy."

When Santa's letter arrived all the elves were very, very busy. Elfalfa sent out a toy making request to the only elf who was free...

BOGGINS!

Elf Boggins looked in
the supply cupboard.
There weren't many
GOOD toy materials
left...

but he tried his hardest
with what he could find.
Then he sent Amy's present
ELFPRESS DELIVERY to Santa.

santa was busy ironing when a very elfish parcel arrived.

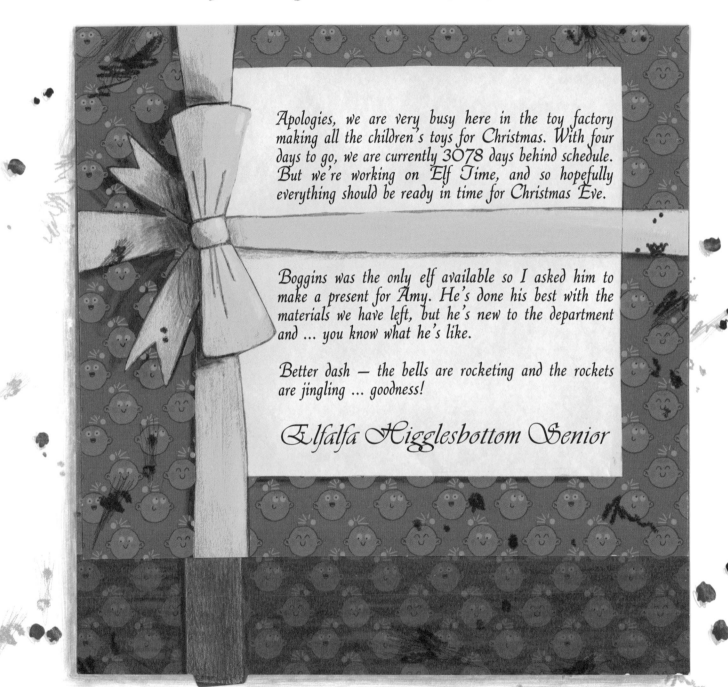

Apologies, we are very busy here in the toy factory making all the children's toys for Christmas. With four days to go, we are currently 3078 days behind schedule. But we're working on Elf Time, and so hopefully everything should be ready in time for Christmas Eve.

Boggins was the only elf available so I asked him to make a present for Amy. He's done his best with the materials we have left, but he's new to the department and ... you know what he's like.

Better dash — the bells are rocketing and the rockets are jingling ... goodness!

Elfalfa Higglesbottom Senior

santa was surprised.

Surely this couldn't be what Amy wanted. She was on the NICE list. "I'll write to Mr Polar Bear," said Santa. "He'll know what Amy wants."

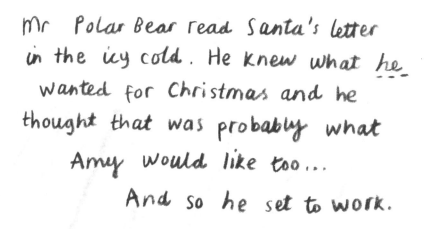

Mr Polar Bear read Santa's letter
in the icy cold. He knew what he
wanted for Christmas and he
thought that was probably what
Amy would like too...

And so he set to work.

He hoped it would be BIG enough for Amy.

Santa was mapping his christmas journey when a GIANT reply arrived.

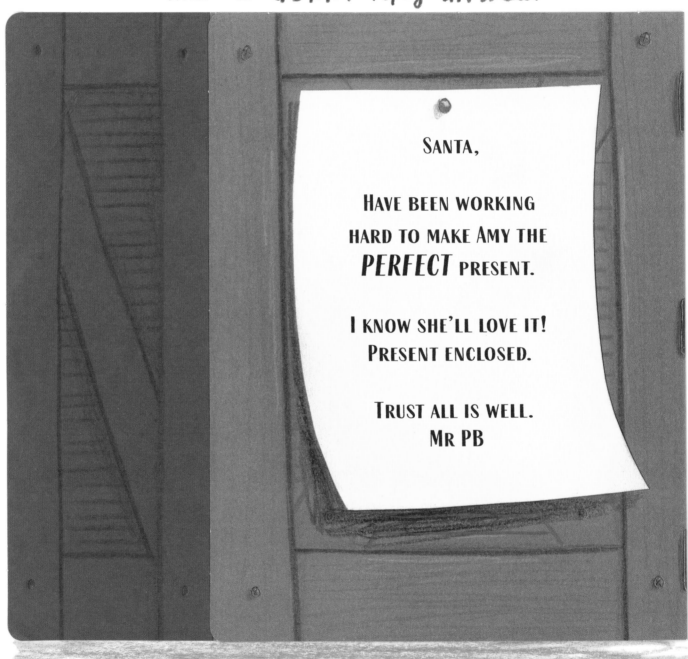

Santa couldn't believe it!

This gift was polar bear-sized!
It wasn't right for Amy and...
it was almost Christmas Eve!
"What can I do?!"
wondered Santa.
"I know, I'll write to the Chief
Reindeer. He's my last hope."

The reindeer were doing some last minute take-off practice when Santa's letter arrived. The Chief Reindeer was very excited to get a letter from Santa Claus.

The Chief Reindeer called
an emergency reindeer
meeting and announced,
"Santa needs us to find
Amy a PRESENT!"

DASHER

COMET

Dancer & Prancer

VIXEN

They put their antlers together and had a BRILLIANT IDEA! It was what they all wanted for christmas.

CUPID

DONNER

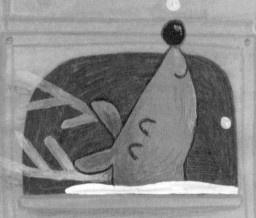

BLITZEN

CHIEF

Santa was stacking presents
when a PARCEL arrived.

Howdy Mister S,
So good to hear from you dude. We've just been surfing some clouds ready for the big night. Dancer dinged her antlers on a star doing an epic dive. It was so awesome. Dasher, Dancer, Prancer, Vixen, Comet, Cupid, Donner, Blitzen and me put our antlers together and have got Amy the best Christmas present ever. She is going to **LOVE** it. Wish I could see your face when you open this parcel. It's gonna blow your mind (and beard).

See ya later!
Peace out.

Chief
The Chief Reindeer

OH NO! This absolutely couldn't be
that Amy wanted most in the
world. But there was no time
left. It was Christmas Eve.
This was the first time in
Christmas history that Santa
had failed to find
someone the right present.
He felt miserable.

There was nothing for it.
Santa filled his sleigh with all the
not-quite-right gifts and soared
into the night sky.
He had a busy night ahead
but all he could think about
was Amy.

NORTH
POLE

At last he arrived at
Amy's chimney, just as
it started to snow.
He looked at the
presents he had brought her.
Santa couldn't give Amy
these gifts...
but what could he do?

Then he had
an idea!

It would take a long time
but he had everything he needed.
It was going to be PERFECT.

Santa spent all of
Christmas Day hoping that
Amy had liked her present.
Then all of a sudden,
the post arrived!
And it was...

SANTA POST!